Mommy's Black Eye

By William George Bentrim

**Bearly
Tolerable
Publications**

Acknowledgements:

Kudos to: My wife for her editing and patience.
             My sister for all her editing, perseverance and inspiration.
             Bob, my golfing buddy who came up with the book title.
             Woman's Place & NOVA (Network of Victim's Assistance)

Author's Note

Domestic violence exists. That is a simple disturbing fact. It isn't something that should be ignored or swept under the rug. It is imperative to face this problem, acknowledge it's existence

and do our best to aid those who are exposed to it. Children, all to often, are susceptible to accepting responsibility for their parents bad behavior. They need to understand that they are not responsible for the violence.   This book attempts to explain a very complicated issue to young children. It is focused on pre-school to middle school children. It is not designed as a panacea, merely an attempt to help them understand what is going on in their lives.

Using a battered mother as an example is not ignoring the fact that men too are abused. Statistics indicate far more mothers are abused than fathers. The gender of the victim is relevant as women are normally the care givers and this greatly limits their alternatives in a domestic violence situation.

This book is not intended to be light hearted but equally I have tried to address domestic violence with a sensitive touch. It is frequently far more disturbing that what is portrayed here. I did not feel that a more graphic portrayal was suitable for the target audience.

Bill

Dedicated to all the victims of domestic violence,
may they survive the experience and
help to eradicate the problem.

Bradley and Bonnie cheerfully waved good bye to their friends, George and Doris Grizzly . They always had a good time at the Grizzly house. Mrs. Grizzly had the biggest honey jar and George and Doris always shared.

Bradley pushed open the door as he and Bonnie arrived home. Bradley was ready to say they were home when he realized it was really dark inside.

All the blinds were down and the lights were off. Peeking in the door, Bonnie yelled, "Mom, are you here?"

They thought they heard a sob and then their mother said, "Kids come in, I'm here."

Bradley went in and said, "Why are all the blinds pulled?

It's like a cave in here."

Mom said, "My eyes are bothering me so I pulled the blinds."

Bradley and Bonnie waited until their eyes adjusted to the light and then they saw Mom sitting in her chair. They went over to hug her and saw she had been crying.

"Mom, how come you're crying," they asked?

Mom said, "It's nothing children, don't worry."

Bradley reached up and turned on the light. "Mom, you have a black eye," he exclaimed!

"Mom, are you ok," Bonnie asked?

Mom started to cry and the kids got scared. "Mom, what's wrong, how come you're crying and why do you have a black eye," they asked?

Mom wiped her tears and said, "I'm really sad, children, your Dad and I had a fight and he hit me," as she started to cry again.

"Does it hurt a lot Mommy," they asked?

Mom said, "No it doesn't hurt too badly but I told your Dad he had to live somewhere else for awhile. That's why I am so sad."

"Why did Dad hit you, were you naughty," Bonnie asked?

"Kids do I hit you when you are naughty," Mom asked?

"No Mom, you give us time outs and sometimes

you take our toys for awhile, but you never hit us. You told us it isn't right to hit other people, just because you are mad," both Bradley and Bonnie said.

"Well, honey, adults shouldn't hit each other when

they are mad either. That's why I told your Dad he had to move out for awhile," Mom said. "Think of it as an adult time out. Maybe if your Daddy has some time to think, he will remember it isn't right to hit other people."

"When can Dad come back? Can I talk to him? Is he going to be mad at us too," Bonnie asked?

"Is he going to hit us too," Bradley asked?

"Children, I don't know when he will come back. Of course you can call and talk to him and no, there is no

reason for him to be mad at you," Mom said. "Daddy is going to have to talk to someone, maybe someone from church or a counselor, who is a person whose job it is to help people work out their problems. If Daddy will do

that, then maybe he and I can meet with a counselor and figure out how we can get along better," Mom said. "Then maybe he can come home again."

"This is really scary Mommy," said both the kids.

"I know it is sweethearts, but we have each other and if Daddy will get some help, maybe we can work it out," said Mom.

"But what if we can't? What if Daddy won't listen to the counselor, what if he wants to hit you again," they asked?

"Then honey, we will have to decide what we want to do. We can't live with someone who wants to hurt us. If Daddy can't change, then we will have to live by ourselves. We have each other and we will be ok if that happens. Maybe we can stay here. Maybe we will have to move but whatever we do, you know I love you and if we are together we will be ok," said Mom.

Bradley and Bonnie were still scared but as Mom hugged them really hard, they knew that they would be ok because they had a Mom who really loved them.

Domestic Abuse Resources

If you or someone you know is in an abusive situation please take action. The following resources should be able to direct you to someone in your own community that can help you, a friend or a loved one. Domestic abuse does not just stop on it's own accord. If you are abused or an abuser, you must take immediate action to remedy the situation.

National Domestic Violence/Child Abuse/ Sexual Abuse 24 hour-a-day hotline:
800-799-SAFE = 800-799-7233
800-787-3224 TDD
800-942-6908 Spanish Speaking

The above numbers provide crisis intervention and referrals to local services and shelters for victims of partner or spousal abuse. English and Spanish speaking advocates are available 24 hours a day, seven days a week. Staffed by trained volunteers who are ready to connect people with emergency help in their own communities, including emergency services and shelters. The staff can also provide information and referrals for a variety of non-emergency services, including counseling for adults and children, and assistance in reporting abuse. They have an extensive database of domestic violence treatment providers in all US states and territories. Many staff members speak languages besides English, and they have 24-hour access to translators for approximately 150 languages. For the hearing impaired, there is a TDD number. This is a great resource for anyone--man, woman or child--who is experiencing or has experienced domestic violence or abuse, or who suspects that someone they know is being abused.

Domestic Violence Hotline: 800-829-1122

USA National Telephone Hotlines
1-800-4-A-CHILD = 1-800-422-4453
ChildHelp USA: Assists any child or teen with any problem including, but not limited to: running away, physical abuse, sexual abuse. Referrals for children, teens, as well as adults. 24 hours.
Web site: http://www.childhelpusa.org

A Clearing House Web Site with a wide variety of resources.
http://www.allaboutcounseling.com/crisis_hotlines.htm

The ACA* recommends 5 ways to help with coping AFTER a crisis situation.

1. Recognize your own feelings about the situation and talk to others about your fears. Know that these feelings are a normal response to an abnormal situation.
2. Be willing to listen to family and friends who have been affected and encourage them to seek counseling if necessary.
3. Be patient with people; fuses are short when dealing with crises and others may be feeling as much stress as you.
4. Recognize normal crises reactions, such as sleep disturbances and nightmares, withdrawal, reverting to childhood behaviors and trouble focusing on work or school.
5. Take time with your children, spouse, life partner, friends and co-workers to do something you enjoy.

*American Counseling Association

CPSIA information can be obtained
at www.ICGtesting.com
Printed in the USA
LVHW071954310522
720136LV00002B/127